READ & BLOOM BOOKS

CAVEBOY
IS A HIT!

SUDIPTA BARDHAN-QUALLEN
ILLUSTRATED BY ERIC WIGHT

BLOOMSBURY
NEW YORK   LONDON   OXFORD   NEW DELHI   SYDNEY

To my favorite caveman, Jim —S. B.-Q.

To Dana, my best teammate —E. W.

Text copyright © 2017 by Sudipta Bardhan-Quallen
Illustrations copyright © 2017 by Eric Wight

First published in the United States of America in December 2017
by Bloomsbury Children's Books
www.bloomsbury.com

Bloomsbury is a registered trademark of Bloomsbury Publishing Plc

For information about permission to reproduce selections from this book, write to
Permissions, Bloomsbury Children's Books, 1385 Broadway, New York, New York 10018
Bloomsbury books may be purchased for business or promotional use. For information on bulk
purchases please contact Macmillan Corporate and Premium Sales Department at
specialmarkets@macmillan.com

Library of Congress Cataloging-in-Publication Data
available upon request
ISBN 978-1-68119-047-1 (hardcover)
ISBN 978-1-68119-129-4 (e-book) • ISBN 978-1-68119-130-0 (e-PDF)

Art created in Photoshop
Typeset in Chaparral Pro, Tiki Island, and House of Terror • Book design by John Candell
Printed in China by C&C Offset Printing Co., Ltd, Shenzhen, Guangdong
1 3 5 7 9 10 8 6 4 2

All papers used by Bloomsbury Publishing, Inc., are natural, recyclable products
made from wood grown in well-managed forests. The manufacturing processes
conform to the environmental regulations of the country of origin.

TABLE OF CONTENTS

CHAPTER 1
OPENING DAY

Caveboy loves a lot of things. He loves his club. He loves his pet rock. He loves his sister, even though she smells like burps. But Caveboy really, really, really loves baseskull.

Today is the first day of baseskull

season. Caveboy is so excited. As soon as the sun rises, he runs out of his cave. He has his club and a bag of brand-new baseskulls. He is ready to go to the baseskull field.

Practice does not start until the sun reaches the top of Tall Mountain. But Caveboy wants to get to the field before anyone else. Practice makes perfect, and more practice makes more perfect!

Caveboy kisses Mama goodbye. "I am going to practice early!" he says. He waves to Papa. He sticks his tongue out at Sister. She sticks her tongue back out at him. Then Caveboy leaves for the field.

The path to the baseskull field goes right past Mags's house. She is outside. But she is not holding her club or a bag of baseskulls. She is lying on the grass, looking up at the clouds.

"Mags!" Caveboy yells. He runs to his friend. "It is the first day of baseskull season. Are you coming to practice?"

Mags sits up. She scratches her head. "I have never played baseskull," she says. "Is it fun?"

Caveboy raises his eyebrow. "Baseskull is my favorite thing!" he cries. "It is so much fun. I have been practicing for baseskull season for a long time."

"Is it hard to play?" Mags asks. "Can you teach me?"

Caveboy grins. "Yes, I can. Practice does not start until the sun reaches the top of Tall Mountain. I can teach you before we go to the field."

Caveboy and Mags move away from her cave. "You do not want to hit your cave with a baseskull. Your parents will not like it." He bites his lip. "My parents never do."

He takes a baseskull out of his bag. "I will throw you a baseskull. You hit it with your club."

"I will try," Mags says.

Caveboy jogs away from Mags. He stands tall with the skull in his hand. He winds up. But there is a problem.

"Ooga booga!" Caveboy shouts.

"Your hands are in the wrong place."

"What do you mean?" Mags asks.

Caveboy jogs back to Mags. "Let me teach you. Hold it at the bottom of the club."

"Now I see," Mags says.

"We can try again," Caveboy says.

"I will throw you a baseskull. You hit it with your club."

He jogs away again.

Caveboy thinks, *Mags needs an easy pitch. She cannot hit a fastskull. She cannot hit a curveskull.* He taps his foot as he thinks. *I will throw the skull slowly. That way, she can hit it easily.*

He stands tall with the skull in his hand. He winds up. But there is another problem.

"Ooga booga!" Caveboy shouts.
He scrunches his eyebrow. "You
are holding your club in a different
wrong way."

"I still do not know how to hold
it," Mags answers.

"I will teach you," Caveboy says. He jogs back to Mags. He is a little out of breath. "You have to hold the bat up," he explains, "because the baseskull will be thrown high, not low."

"I get it now," Mags says.

"We can try again," Caveboy pants. He jogs away again. He stands tall with the skull in his hand again. He winds up again. But there is another, new problem.

"OOGA BOOGA!"
Caveboy shouts. He
rolls his eyes. "You
are still holding your
club the wrong way!"

"But I think I
see a spider!" Mags
shrieks.

Caveboy jogs back
to Mags. He is very
out of breath. "Where?" he asks.
"Where is this spider?"

"Right there," Mags says.

Caveboy looks and looks, then he rolls his eyes.

"That is not a spider! That is just a hairball from a mammoth!"

Mags blushes. "Sorry," she says. "It really did look like a big, mean spider. While you are here, show me how to hold my club."

"You have to hold it like this,"
Caveboy explains, "because you have
to hit the baseskull as far as you can,
not thump it into the ground."

"I get it now," Mags says.

Caveboy does not say anything. He is bent over, breathing hard.

"Are you too tired to try again?" Mags asks.

Caveboy shakes his head. He takes a few big breaths. Then he says, "No, I am not too tired. We can try again." He jogs away again. He stands tall with the skull in his hand again. He winds up again. This time, he throws the pitch.

Mags pulls her club back and then . . .

 **17**

SWING! BOOM!

The skull flies up, up, up. Caveboy runs to get under it. He catches it.

But Mags is squealing, "I did it! I hit a baseskull!" She hugs Caveboy. "You taught me how!"Caveboy is happy that his friend is happy. So he thinks, *I will teach her about outs . . . later.*

CHAPTER 2
PITCHING PRACTICE

Mags is very excited about her hit. "Time for baseskull practice!" she announces.

Caveboy shakes his head. "There is still more to teach you."

"But the sun!" Mags says. She

points. "It is almost at the top of Tall Mountain."

Mags is right. Practice will start soon. "We should go then," Caveboy agrees.

Soon, Caveboy and Mags arrive at the field. A coach calls them over. "Let's get started," he shouts.

There are two other cavekids with the coach already. Caveboy does not know either of them.

"I am Coach Bill," the coach says. "Tell me your names."

"I am Caveboy," Caveboy says, "and this is Mags."

The cavekid with dark, curly hair says, "My name is Grub."

"I am Fish," says the one with yellow hair. She is wearing a seashell necklace.

"I am happy to meet you all,"
Coach Bill says. "Are you excited
about baseskull?"

Caveboy and Fish shout, "YES!"

"Are you nervous?" Coach Bill
asks.

"Yes," Mags mumbles. Grub
mumbles yes, too.

"Do not be nervous!" Coach Bill
says. "Some of you are already good

baseskull players. And some of you are just starting. But we are all going to learn a lot this season."

Caveboy elbows Mags. "See?" he says. "You are not the only new player."

"Did you all bring baseskulls?" Coach Bill asks.

All the other cavekids shake their heads. So Caveboy says, "I brought many baseskulls. We can all share mine."

Coach Bill smiles. "You are already thinking like a teammate! Good job."

Caveboy gives everyone a thumbs-up.

"Today, we will work on running, pitching, and hitting," Coach Bill continues.

Caveboy grins a giant grin. "I am a good runner," he says to Mags. "And I am a good pitcher. And I am a very good hitter!"

But Mags does not grin back.

Caveboy scrunches his eyebrow.
"What is wrong, Mags?"

Mags frowns. "I am a good
runner," she says.

"Yes, you are!" Caveboy agrees.

Mags nods. "But I have only ever hit a baseskull once. And I have never pitched at all." She sighs. "Is this a good idea?"

"Of course it is, Mags!" Caveboy replies. "Baseskull is so much fun, I promise."

"Time to run!" Coach Bill announces. "You will run from here to the Twisted Tree. Then you turn left and run to the Double Stump."

The players line up at the starting
line. Coach Bill yells,

One . . . two . . . three . . . GO!

Mags runs and runs. Caveboy runs

and runs. Fish and Grub run and run. Mags is very fast. Caveboy is faster. But Grub is even faster than that. He reaches the Double Stump first. Caveboy is second.

"I won! I won!" Grub shouts. He dances to celebrate.

"You are very fast," Caveboy says.

Grub grins. "But you almost beat me," he says. "Next time, you will probably win."

Caveboy smiles.

Coach Bill congratulates them. "Good job!" he says. "You all did great. But keep practicing!"

Grub beams at the coach. But Fish stares at the ground. Mags kicks the dirt with her feet. They do not look like they want to practice anymore.

Coach Bill shouts, "Time to hit!" He climbs onto the pitcher's mound. The players line up at home plate.

Fish is the first one up. She pulls her club back and then . . .

SWING! BOOM!

"Great hit!" Mags shouts.

Fish grins from ear to ear.

Next is Grub. Coach Bill throws

the pitch and . . .

SWING! THUMP!

Grub scowls. "Try again," Fish yells.

Grub gets ready to hit and then . . .

SWING! BOOM!

"Another great hit!" Caveboy shouts.

Grub smiles and gives Fish a high five.

Then it is Caveboy's turn. He taps the ground with his club. He holds it up. He nods to show he is ready.

The pitch comes at him and . . .

SWING! BOOM!

"That was a fantastic hit!" Mags cheers.

Caveboy grins.

It is Mags's turn last. Coach Bill pitches the ball.

SWING! THUMP!

"Try again," Grub says.

Coach Bill pitches again.

SWING! THUMP!

"Keep trying, Mags!" Caveboy shouts.

Mags narrows her eyes. She holds her club up. She keeps her eyes on the baseskull.

Coach Bill throws another pitch.

SWING! THUMP!

"Good try, Mags," Coach Bill says. "You just need more practice. We all need to keep practicing."

Mags looks away.

"Everybody misses sometimes," Caveboy says. "Do not feel bad."

Mags squeezes her eyes shut. "Today, I was not good at running. I was not good at hitting. And I will probably not be good at pitching."

"But, Mags," Fish says, "I was not so good at running, either."

"And I was not so good at hitting," Grub adds.

A small tear trickles down Mags's cheek. "Fish, you were not so good at running. But you were very good at hitting. Grub, you were great at running. And you were a better hitter than me. And, Caveboy, you were good at everything." She sniffles.

"Mags," Caveboy says, "we are going to be a team. That means we do not all have to be good at everything." He pats her on the shoulder.

Fish and Grub nod. They agree with Caveboy.

"Being teammates also means we will help one another," Caveboy continues. "Do not give up, Mags! We all have to keep practicing. Practice makes perfect, and more practice makes more perfect!"

Mags shakes her head. "Maybe baseskull is not for me."

"It is time to pitch!" Coach Bill shouts. He points to a target he has

drawn on a tree trunk. "Try to hit the bull's-eye with the baseskull," he says. "Do your best."

The players line up to pitch. Mags is at the back of the line.

During Fish's turn and Grub's turn, Caveboy tries to think of ways to make Mags feel better. That is when he sees a small spider crawl across Coach Bill's foot. He peeks

back at Mags to make sure she does not see. She hates spiders.

Suddenly, Caveboy has a great idea!

"Caveboy," Coach Bill calls. "You are up!"

Caveboy forgot it was his turn. He runs to the mound and pitches. He is too quick and sloppy. The baseskull does not even come close to the tree. But Caveboy runs off the mound before Coach Bill can say keep practicing. He goes back to Mags.

Mags is squeezing her baseskull so hard her fingers are turning white. Her hand is trembling a bit. "It is your turn," Caveboy whispers.

Mags gulps. Then she steps on the pitching mound. She stretches her neck. Then she rolls her shoulders. Finally, she draws her hand back.

Then Caveboy shouts, "Mags! Is that a spider on your baseskull?"

"A spider!" Mags screeches. She throws the baseskull away as hard as she can. It flies through the air until . . .

THWACK!

Caveboy cannot believe it. "Ooga booga! Look, Mags!" He points.

"Is it gone?" Mags asks. She is hiding her eyes. She does not see what Caveboy sees.

Caveboy grabs her hands. He turns her around and makes her look. "You hit the target!" There is a hole where the target should be. The baseskull went through the target *and* the tree!

"Try it again," Coach Bill says. He hands Mags another baseskull.

Mags clutches the baseskull. She pulls her arm back. Then Caveboy shouts, "Spider!"

She pitches again. This time, she throws the baseskull harder than the first time.

"Mags, you are the best pitcher on the field!" Grub shouts. Everyone cheers for Mags.

"Thank you, Caveboy," says Mags. "You figured out the trick to help me pitch."

"You are a good teammate," Coach Bill says.

"And a good friend," Mags adds.

Caveboy blushes. But he is happy to help Mags. "Come on," he says, "we have to keep practicing!"

CHAPTER 3
LOST AND FOUND

At the end of practice, the cavekids
are tired.

"You all did very well today," Coach
Bill announces. "I will see you again
in two suns for our next practice.
Now go home and get some rest!"

"Can you all help me collect my baseskulls?" Caveboy asks.

"Of course!" Grub answers. Mags and Fish nod.

They gather the baseskulls and put them back in the bag.

When they are done, it is time to go home. Caveboy and Mags wave goodbye.

Grub says, "See you in two suns!"

Caveboy, Mags, and Grub start to walk away. But Fish does not move. "I cannot go home!" she cries.

Caveboy scrunches his eyebrow. "Why not?" he asks.

"I have lost my necklace!" she replies. "My mother will be so angry!"

"I remember seeing it when we started practice," Caveboy says.

"Then I took it off," Fish says. "I put it with our clubs when we started running." She points to the bench. "But it is not there anymore!"

"Do not worry, Fish," Mags says. "We will help you find your necklace."

Caveboy and Grub nod. Caveboy says, "It will be in the last place we look."

The cavekids all start to search.
Grub looks behind the rock bench.
Caveboy looks around the pitcher's
mound. Mags looks on top of the
Double Stump.

Then Fish shouts, "I think I see it!"
She points to a giant mushroom. "Is
that a seashell?"

They all move closer to the
giant mushroom. Then Caveboy
says, "Stop! That is not a seashell.
Seashells do not move. That is a
snail."

"You are right, Caveboy," Grub
says.

"But do not worry, Fish," Mags adds, "we will keep looking."

They all search again. Caveboy looks near an empty termite mound. Mags looks in a muddy puddle. Fish looks in the tall grass.

Then Grub shouts, "I think I see it!" He points to a leafy bush. "Is that a seashell?"

They all move closer to the bush.
Then Caveboy shouts, "STOP! That
is not a seashell. Seashells are not
scaly. That is a snake!"

When the snake is gone, Fish says, "We still have not found my necklace."

"Do not worry, Fish," Grub says. "We will still help you look."

This time, Grub looks behind the leafy bush. Fish looks under a broken branch. Caveboy looks inside a hole in the Twisted Tree.

Then Mags shouts, "I think I see it!" She points to a big boulder. "Is that a seashell?"

They go to the boulder. Mags
reaches up for the necklace. But
something does not look right to
Caveboy. He scratches his head.

Then he hisses, "Mags, STOP! That is not a seashell!"

Mags turns around. "What do you mean?"

"Seashells are not furry."

"Then what is it?" Mags asks

"Is it a snail?" Grub asks.

Caveboy says, "I do not think so. Snails do not have fur."

"Is it a snake?" Fish asks.

Caveboy says, "I do not think so. Snakes have scales, not fur."

"What could it be?" Mags asks.

"It is a saber-tooth tiger!"

AHHHHHHHHH!

Fish lowers her eyes. "We are safe,

but . . ." She sniffles. "But we have
not found my necklace. And that
was the last place to look. Now there

is nowhere left." She sniffles again. "My necklace is gone forever!"

Mags puts her arm around Fish's shoulders. Grub says, "It will be all right, Fish."

Fish is very upset. Caveboy does not know how to make her feel better. *I want to do something nice for her*, he thinks.

Then he has a great idea! He will give Fish one of his special, new baseskulls. He grabs his bag. He digs through trying to find one that is not scuffed or dirty. *I want to find a really nice one*, he thinks.

And then Caveboy shouts, "Ooga booga!"

"What has happened?" Mags asks.

Caveboy slaps his forehead. "We did not look for Fish's necklace in the last place. The last place was not on top of the boulder. The last place was my baseskull bag," he says.

He pulls something out of the bag. "This is not a baseskull. I am sorry," he mumbles. "I must have put it away by accident."

Fish takes her necklace. Her mouth falls open. And then she cheers, "Thank you, Caveboy!"

 **68**

"But I was the one who lost it,"
Caveboy mumbles. "Are you mad?"

Fish shakes her head. "You found
it. That is all that matters to me."

Caveboy grins. "I told you we

would find your necklace in the last place we looked!" He laughs. Then he pulls Fish, Grub, and Mags into a group hug. "I also found something more important," he says. "I found more good friends!"

READ & BLOOM

PLANT THE LOVE OF READING!

Agnes and
Clarabelle are the
best of friends!

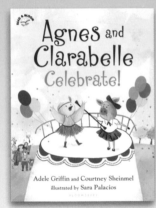

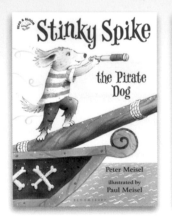

Stinky Spike can
sniff his way out
of any trouble!

You don't want to miss these great characters! The Read & Bloom line is perfect for newly independent readers. These stories are fully illustrated and bursting with fun!

Caveboy is always ready for an adventure!

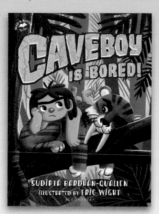

Wallace and Grace are owl detectives who solve mysteries!

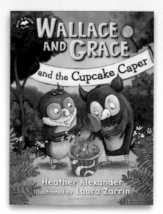

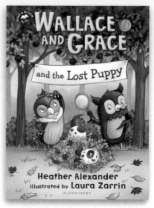

 www.bloomsbury.com • Twitter: BloomsburyKids • Facebook: KidsBloomsbury

SUDIPTA BARDHAN-QUALLEN lives in New Jersey with her cavefamily—three cavekids and one cavehusband. She cannot hit baseskulls, hunt saber-tooth tigers, or scare away spiders, but she is very good at reading, traveling, and shopping for shoes. Sudipta is the award-winning author of over forty books for children, including *Duck, Duck, Moose!*, *Tyrannosaurus Wrecks!*, and *Chicks Run Wild*.

sudipta.com

ERIC WIGHT spends a lot of time in his cave making books for children, including the Frankie Pickle and Magic Shop series. When he was a kid, he had a unibrow just like Caveboy. He lives with his wife and herd of children in Chalfont, Pennsylvania.

ericwight.com